RACE RESULTS

SATURN
6TH PLACE

URANUS
7TH PLACE

NEPTUNE
8TH PLACE

PLUTO
9TH PLACE

To my out-of-this-world sister, Pat —R.S.

To Sarah C., your love for three —B.W.

*The editors would like to thank Amie Gallagher,
Planetarium Director at Raritan Valley Community College,
for her assistance in the preparation of this book.*

Text copyright © 2015 by Rob Sanders
Jacket art and interior illustrations copyright © 2015 by Brian Won

Visit us on the Web! randomhousekids.com

Educators and librarians, for a variety of teaching tools, visit us at RHTeachersLibrarians.com

Library of Congress Cataloging-in-Publication Data
Sanders, Rob.
Outer space bedtime race / by Rob Sanders ; illustrated by Brian Won. — First edition.
pages cm.
Summary: "Aliens from all planets race to complete their quirky
bedtime routines." —Provided by publisher.
ISBN 978-0-385-38647-0 (trade) — ISBN 978-0-375-97354-3 (lib. bdg.) —
ISBN 978-0-385-38648-7 (ebook)
[1. Stories in rhyme. 2. Bedtime—Fiction. 3. Planets—Fiction. 4. Extraterrestrial beings—Fiction.]
I. Won, Brian, illustrator. II. Title.
PZ8.3.S22420u 2015 [E]—dc23 2014011538

Book design by John Sazaklis

MANUFACTURED IN CHINA   10 9 8 7 6 5 4 3 2 1 First Edition

OUTER ★ SPACE
BEDTIME RACE

by **ROB SANDERS**

illustrated by **BRIAN WON**

Finn—
Should you
ever want a
destination—
look to the
skies!
Rob Sanders

RANDOM HOUSE 🏠 NEW YORK

"Good night! Good night!" the children call
while spinning on their earthly ball.
They pull their covers way up tight
and turn off every bedside light.

Tucked safely in their comfy beds,
they're not the only sleepyheads.
In outer space it's bedtime, too.
The aliens need sleep like you.

Those aliens zip round the sun.

The time for racing has begun.

The planets line up in a row.

Now ready, set, and blast off . . .

GO!

The Mercury kids land rocket ships,
then hurry to their nightly dips.
They glide along on rocky paths
to steamy crater bubble baths.

Inside sleep chambers, warm and snug, they squeeze together in a hug.

Click-CLICK go all the chamber lids. It's bedtime for the Mercury kids.

On Venus, time goes on and on—
it seems like days and days till dawn.
Kids shimmy into deep-sleep suits
and rubberized compression boots.

They sip on warm Galactic Goop
and slurp the slime chunks, scoop by scoop.
As satellites go whizzing by,
loud snores from Venus fill the sky.

The Martians scrub and wash and clean,
and soon their skin is gleaming green.
They rinse and spit with Martian flair,
then comb their tangled, star-filled hair.

They *boing* and *bounce* on giant springs
and land inside red hammock swings.
The Martian parents softly hum
when slumber-time on Mars has come.

To fall asleep on Jupiter,

the kids count moons till their eyes blur.

They use twelve fingers and six toes,

till finally they start to doze.

The rings of Saturn circle round
as Saturn kids at last bed down.
They rest their heads on clouds of fluff.
Get this—they all sleep in the buff!

Uranus is a gassy place.

They sleep with masks stuck to each face.

Before lights-out, with beaks in books,

they curl up inside cozy nooks.

Since Neptune swarms with icy clouds,
the Neptunites must sleep in crowds.
Just as the clock strikes fifty-nine,
those snoozers cross the finish line.

FINISH

The Pluto kids sleep on their feet,
lined up together, nice and neat.
Poor Pluto is so very small,
it's not a planet after all.

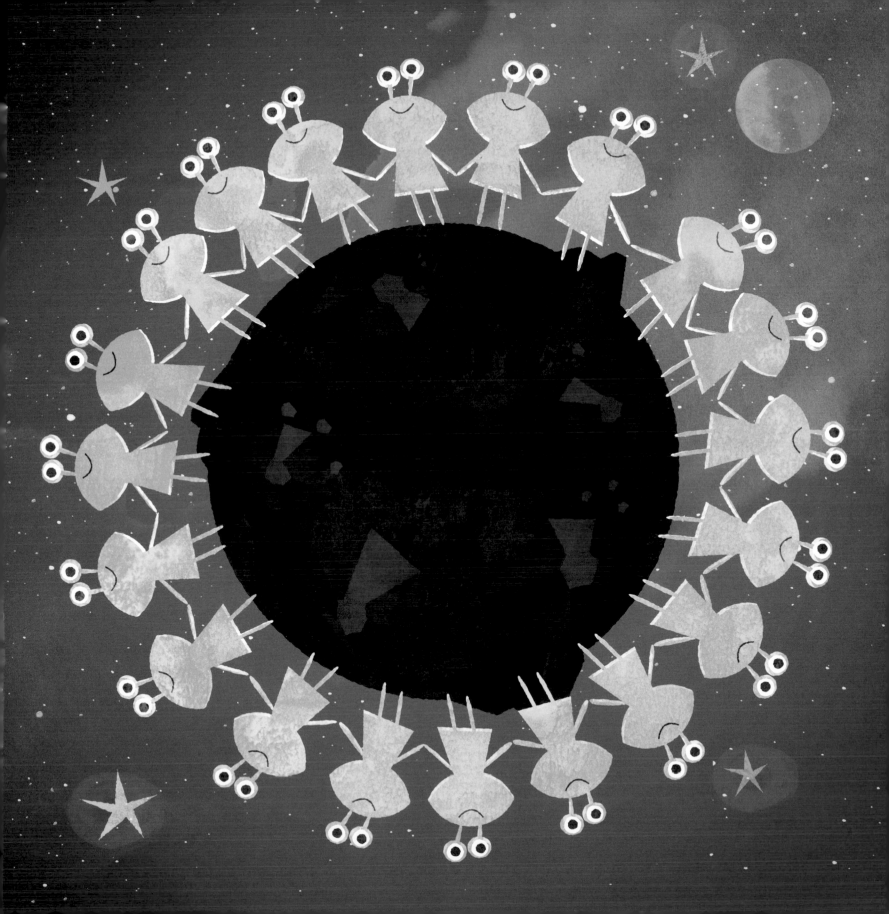

The aliens are now asleep,
out in the cosmos dark and deep.
They end their nightly bedtime race
as planets spin through outer space.

Far from the starry Milky Way,
where asteroids zigzag and sway,
past comets and a shooting star,
and all the way to where you are . . .

. . . this Outer Spacy Bedtime Race

has now returned to our home base.

With all the aliens in bed,

it's now *your* turn, you sleepyhead.

SLEEPY BEDTIME PLANET FACTOIDS

THE SUN

The sun is the real star of our solar system. This giant ball of gases is more than a million times larger than Earth. Now, that's big! All the planets in our solar system orbit around the sun. It also provides heat to Earth. Without it, bedtime would be *ch-ch-chilly*!

MERCURY

Mercury bubble baths would be steamy since the temperature on this planet, which is closest to the sun, can reach 801°F during the day. But be sure to wear your warmest deep-sleep suit at bedtime. Temperatures at night can fall to -290°F.

VENUS

One day on Venus is as long as 243 Earth days. That's about eight months from sunrise to sunrise! Now you know that the days there are *l-o-n-g*.

EARTH

Earth is the only planet in the solar system known to support life. When you fall asleep tonight, you will be joining millions of other human beings who also sleep on Planet Earth.

MARS

Scientists know that water once flowed on Mars. But now the planet is like a frozen desert. So if you're planning to brush your teeth there, you might have to rinse with dusty Martian air!

JUPITER

Jupiter has over sixty moons. Try counting all those! You'll need more than just your fingers and your toes, and you'll probably fall asleep before you finish.

SATURN

The rings of Saturn are made up of billions of large and small chunks of ice, but are only about one hundred feet thick! Clouds swirl on Saturn, the second-largest planet in the solar system. I hope the kids there hold on tightly to their clouds!

URANUS

Uranus has no solid surface and is made up mostly of gas. The gas gives the planet its blue-green color. And get this: Uranus is tipped over sideways! That means it spins like a ball rolling on the ground, not like a dancer twirling.

NEPTUNE

Hurricane-like winds often blow across Neptune, "the blue planet." Neptune takes the equivalent of 165 Earth years to orbit the sun. That's more than 60,000 bedtimes on Earth. I'm tired just thinking about it!

PLUTO

In 2006, Pluto officially became an *un*-planet. Because of its small size and irregular orbit, Pluto was classified as a *dwarf planet*. There are four other known dwarf planets in the solar system. Pluto may be small, but it's not alone.

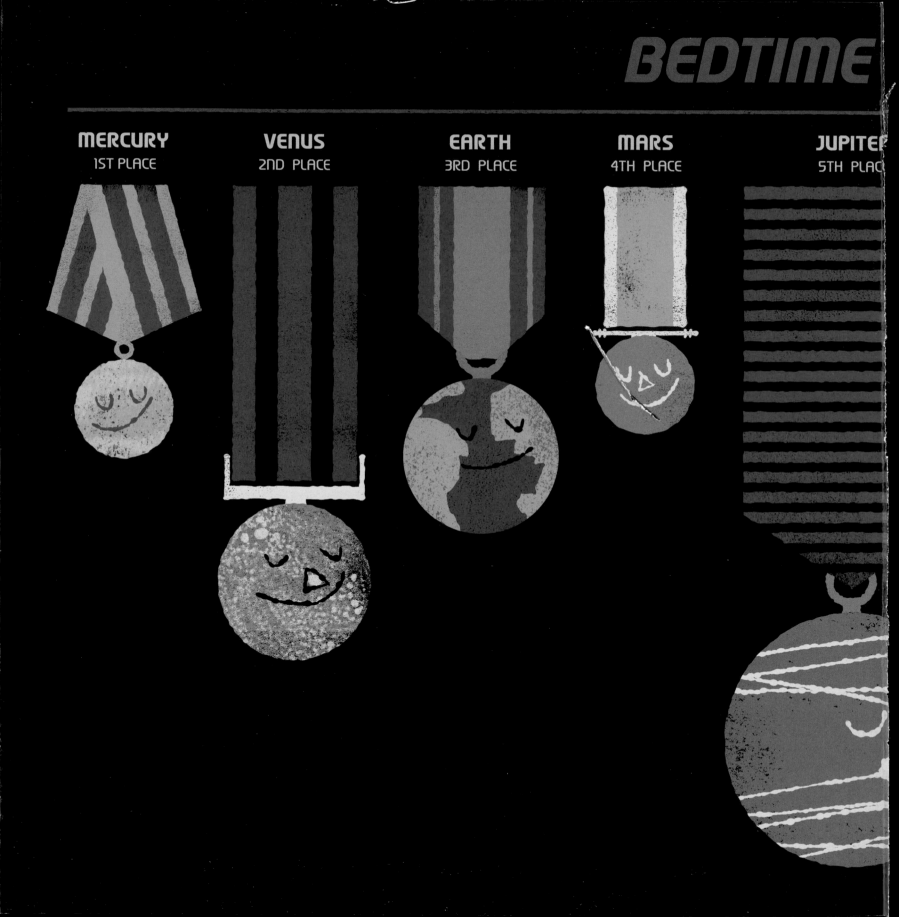